THE HAMSTER OF HAMPSTEAD HEATH

BY MARTIN PLAUT

Illustrations by Mike Spoor

With thanks to all the men and women whose tireless efforts keep Hampstead Heath and Kenwood the wonderful resource that they are, for all Londoners to share and enjoy, even the smallest!

ISBN 978-1-84728-285-9

Introduction to Hampstead Heath
by Vole

At the centre of the Known Universe lie the great lakes, fed by the mighty Fleet River. Hamster and I have residences to the west of the most spectacular lake that is home to many ducks and swans. On the opposite shore is a vast grassy prairie. Our burrows are built into a range of towering hills that gradually descends to the south. To our north lie forests and a great and mysterious house, known as Kenwood.

Over years of exploration by many of my braver ancestors, it has been established that beyond the edges of our world (which is called by us Hampstead Heath) are endless barren wastes known as "London". Here live vicious cats, packs of dogs and hordes of humans. From our highest hills the brick and concrete of London stretch as far as the eye can see.

One estimate suggests that the Heath covers nearly 800 acres, but this is beyond the imagination of all, and seems highly improbable. The origins of the Heath are unknown, but popular mythology suggests that one Baroness Burdett-Coutts, the daughter of the richest banker, preserved the Heath from encroachment by developers in the 1880's. Festivals celebrating her good works abound, and her sacred memory is venerated by all who live on the Heath.

In 1989 a celestial body known as the "City of London" is believed to have taken control of the management of the Heath. The nature and importance of this organisation are still being investigated.

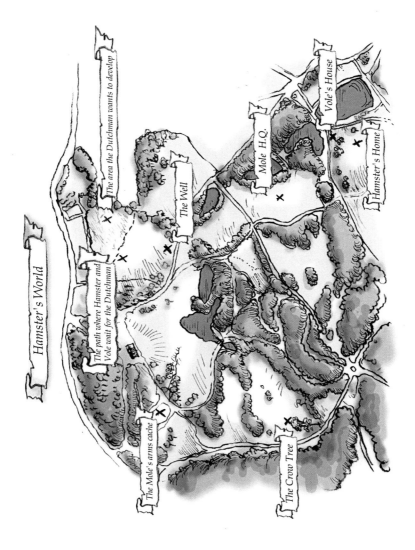

Hamster's World

The area the Dutchman wants to develop

The Well

Mole H.Q.

Vole's House

Hamster's Home

The path where Hamster and Vole wait for the Dutchman

The Mole's arms cache

The Crow Tree

Hamster woke with a start.

The sun, going down behind the hill, had sent its last ray past the root, between the rocks, into his burrow. It caught him on the face. "Who's shining that light?" he called out, and felt a little silly when no reply came.

Hamster had been snuggled into his favourite chair, but somehow its familiar shape, with its lumps and bumps of long use were of little comfort. The memories of what he had seen and heard the day before kept crowding into his mind. A menace seemed to hang in the air.

"Well, off to Vole," he muttered to himself. "Vole's a sensible chap. He'll know what to do."

Hamster pulled on his long, tweed coat and his favourite silk scarf (inherited from his great great-grandfather, who had brought it back from no-one dares ask where) and went out, just as the sun finally said its farewells and rode off into the night.

It was still warm enough. He walked briskly along the well worn path, over the mound and down to the pond. The ducks were still very much at work.

"Greedy, fat, hopeless. As if they don't get enough bread flung at them every day!" Then he reflected. At least they weren't Canada Geese. Now there were a really unstoppable lot. "They'd eat the world flat," he said out loud.

But before he got much further, he arrived at Vole's house.

Now Vole's was snug. A bit too snug for Hamster, especially with his overcoat and padded waistcoat on, but he squeezed through the doorway, and down the narrow passage, until it widened out into Vole's sitting room.

"Well, really!" Hamster muttered. "He doesn't get tidier with time!" And it was true. Everywhere the room was crammed with boats. Boats of every description. From common or garden punts, to grand galleons and clippers fit to sail around the Horn. They were crowded on the mantelpiece, displayed in glass cabinets, hung from the ceiling. Indeed, it was hard to see what space there was left to live in.

And there in his corner was the slight figure of Vole himself. By the light of a lantern he was busily working away. A Venetian gondola, no less, was emerging from a mass of balsa, wire, paper and fixative. It was a messy business, and Vole was so immersed, it was only when Hamster was almost upon him that he sat upright with a start.

"Oh!" he said. "Oh, it's you, Hamster."

"Yes. And I've come on a mission. Perhaps the most important we've ever faced. So put down your craft and pay attention."

* * *

Hamster lowered himself into the only chair that was unoccupied, folded his arms and stared at the ceiling.

"It was on Sunday," he said. "I was at home, minding my own business, when this cellophane came wafting into my burrow. Worse than that, it was followed by a cloud of green-grey smoke."

He winced at the memory.

"Cigar smoke. Disgusting in the extreme. And there, just on the other side of the great fence, were two men. The one was Dutch, the one with the cigar. The other was English. Town dressed as country, if you know what I mean."

"They were talking, rather quietly. But I cocked an ear and what do you know! They're planning to seize our land! Our land! Been safe for generations. Ever since that banking woman, bless her kindly ways, secured it in time out of mind. But now they're back. Those developers, with their plans. And they don't mean to be stopped!"

Vole stared at Hamster in disbelief. It was too terrible, if true, but he was not the sort to be thrown by the news.

* * *

Vole, who until then had been picking bits of glue off his cuffs, got up.

"Tea first, then we can think," he said and disappeared behind an embroidered curtain that hung across the minute closet that served as his kitchen.

It was some time before he reappeared, but Hamster was used to his ways. "Needs time to take it all in," he said to himself. With a clattering of china, Vole returned, putting down the tray on the legs that were folded neatly beneath it.

"Well, there's only one thing for it," he finally said, when they'd both had two cups of tea and a buttered crumpet each.

Hamster looked expectant, but was not ready for the suggestion when it finally came. "The Crow," said Vole, staring into the fire.

It wasn't much, but Hamster reacted as if he'd been stung. "Out of the question! Quite out of the question!" He was on his feet, waving his saucer at Vole. "Not been done in this generation! Do you know the dangers? Have you heard the tales? Quite out of the question!"

Vole said nothing. He just looked up at the clutter that hung from the ceiling, as if nothing was taking place. Eventually Hamster subsided and slumped back into his chair.

"Well!" he said. "Well, if you're sure. No other remedy?" He looked hopefully at his friend, but Vole said nothing.

"Well, then I suppose the Crow it is. I'd better be off home and pack. Be with you at last light."

It was with a heavy heart that Hamster made his way out of Vole's home and over the path. He even looked with some affection in the direction of the ducks, now paddling on the still pond. When might he see them again?

* * *

Vole padded about, clearing away the tea things after Hamster left.

Strange cove, he said to himself, as he wiped the cups dry. You could never quite tell with him. Who would have thought that he could be so exercised by this threat?

Vole went back to his gondola, but although he fiddled about with a seat he was making, his thoughts kept drifting back to Hamster.

"Perhaps it's the past," he said out loud at last, thinking back to how they'd met.

He remembered that night, so long ago, when he'd gone to his door to answer the insistent knocking. It had been raining, and there was Hamster, drenched to the bone. His thin coat was sticking to his sides, an old hat dripped water onto his face. A tatty scarf was wound around his neck and his shoes were covered in mud.

Vole had had such a shock, he'd almost slammed the door on this dismal figure. But there was something about the hamster's downcast expression that stopped him. Soon Hamster was sitting in his underwear, in front of the fire, his clothes steaming on a rack.

Gently, Vole had pried his story from him. The horror of the big house. The torture of being trapped behind bars day and night....Hamster was reluctant to go into details, but he shivered, despite the log fire blazing in front of him.

"And finally, I saw my chance. I was let out, to exercise on the carpet. Before me were the curtains, high as a cliff. I didn't know how, but I knew I must get out," Hamster had told him.

Up he'd gone, and seeing a narrow window, he'd jumped. Luckily for him, there was a thick hydrangea bush below to cushion his fall. From then, he'd been on the run. Onto the Heath he'd come, hotly chased by children and dogs. That was three days ago, and he had been at his wits end; cold, hungry and miserable, when he'd seen the light beneath Vole's door.

It had all taken place years ago, but somehow it seemed to explain Hamster's behaviour today. Vole got up, and pushed the gondola to one side. "Perhaps," he thought to himself, "Perhaps it's because he's a refugee. He's an exile in a strange land. He's made his life here, and that's why he's now so disturbed by this threat. There's no going home for him!"

* * *

Hamster was well kitted out by the time he returned. On his back he carried his rucksack, with a groundsheet tucked underneath and an umbrella protruding from the top. Hamster was always pessimistic about the weather and never keen to get wet. "Does dreadful things to the fur," he used to say. There was tea in a flask, sandwiches and some chocolate bars, with hazelnuts.

Vole was rather more lightly attired. True, he had an anorak and a sou'wester, but the kit bag over his shoulder contained only one item that might be considered an extravagance: a notebook. Vole was meticulous about detail and he felt sure any conversation with the Crow should be carefully preserved (if they ever got that far).

"Off we go, then" said Hamster, putting on his-best-foot-forward face. Vole was struggling to keep up as they crossed the swampy ground behind the burrow. It was early spring and they made their way under the yellow heads of the daffodils that hung in clusters on the slope. The stream was running briskly. It was no obstacle for Vole, although Hamster never quite got used to crossing the log that bridged the stream.

There before them lay the Long Grassy Hill. Two old Russians were making their way slowly up the hill. She led the way, scolding her husband for being slow, while he dragged his feet, his hat pulled down on his head, wishing for his fireplace.

After they disappeared, Hamster and Vole had the place to themselves. The night was all around them now as they made progress by stages, until finally they arrived at the brambles marking the edge of the wood.

* * *

To the two travellers, the sharp thorns and twisted stems ahead were a wall of barbed wire. But a careful reconnoitre revealed a rabbit-way through the seemingly impenetrable thicket. Now rabbits may be silly, but they have all the requirements of good engineers: they are persistent, energetic, resourceful and, above all, they are numerous. Once rabbits put their minds to getting through the brambles, they go to it with a will. They choose their moment, when most of the shoots are still young and tender in Spring, and carve a path through the undergrowth. And, as old rabbits are wont to say, "Once made, always ready."

For Hamster and Vole the tunnel had its drawbacks. Having entered it, they were effectively trapped and there was little option but to go on. So when the sharp scent of a ferret wafted towards them on the night breeze, there was little they could do but step up their pace. The tunnel twisted and turned, but finally they were at its end. Beyond lay the wood floor, with its piles of decomposing leaves.

Vole felt tired and dispirited, but he said nothing. It was all a very long way from the water's edge. "I know what he'll say, if I complain," he thought to himself. "Well, whose idea was it to set off to see the Crow? And he'd be right. So better keep my thoughts to myself."

Hamster too was getting fed up. But they pressed ahead, around holly bushes that towered above them, past rhododendron stumps (killed off as a foreign invader—no doubt to warn others!) until, just as they were about to give up hope, the stars twinkled ahead of them through a gap in the oaks and they knew they were close to their goal. They sat on a clump of grass on the edge of the wood to eat their sandwiches.

* * *

"Well," said Hamster. "When the sun comes up over that hill, fate will be upon us!"

Vole wondered where Hamster got phrases like that, but he knew better than to comment. Hamster read too much, he always felt, and digested too little. "How do you think," he ventured instead, "we can get to the Crow, without his escort taking us for enemies and tearing down on us?"

"Only one thing for it. Use the dock leaf strategy."

Ancient though it might have been, they both knew what that meant. Anyone carrying a dock leaf over his head comes in peace. Perhaps it was because they were so bulky that they made any possibility of springing a surprise on a foe next to impossible. Perhaps it was because of their healing properties. In any event, they were recognised by all concerned as giving protection to anyone who held them high.

So it was, as the first rays of the morning sun pierced the branches of the trees on the hill before them, that the two made their way—a little fearfully—out of the safety of the wood. With dock leaves over their heads almost obscuring them from view, they made their way towards the foot of the great beech tree.

* * *

No sooner were they out of the protective canopy of the wood, than the escort was upon them. Swooping from the skies above, they bore down on the two friends, who cowered beneath the flimsy protection of their leaves. Wings pounded the air. Talons whistled past their heads. One of the crows of the Elite Escort Division made passes over them, skimming above them by a fur's breadth.

"Kaaar. Kaaar. Kaar."

The hill resounded to the cries of the crows as they wheeled over their prey. But even they, even these merciless villains of the Heath, could not quite bring themselves to rip aside the leaves and split their prey asunder.

"Saaaow," he finally said. "Saaaow. What do we have here? Two miserable specimens, and no mistake. And what might they be doing on the mount? Daaock leaves and all? Caaam on. Out with it. Whaaat do you want?"

Hamster, normally so eloquent, found his throat too parched to speak. Finally it was Vole who plucked up courage. "Advice," was all he managed.

"Aaahow! Advice is it! And free advice I suppose?" questioned the crow.

"Yes," quivered Hamster, who'd finally managed to open his throat. "We are all in danger. We are. Even you are. It's a threat we can't ignore. So we came for advice. Only the Crow has the wisdom we need!"

"Aaahow, yes. Aaahow yes. Wisdom he has. But what's this about danger. We laaave danger. Not afraid, not a bit of it. Lot of raaabbish, sounds to me. Still, can't be too caaareful."

And with that he signalled to two guards. In an instant the Hamster and Vole were seized by there rucksacks, pulled off the ground and were soaring into the skies.

* * *

They were flung down into a nest, and it was none-too-soft a landing. The nest was made of twigs and branches and less than scrupulously clean. As they picked themselves up, the first thing they saw were two scraggy, almost naked legs. Above them loomed grey, withered feathers. The Crow seemed asleep, his beak under his wing, guarded on either side by tall, muscular bodyguards who glared down at the pair.

Neither Hamster nor Vole knew quite what to do. But finally Hamster drew himself up and addressed the ancient bird.

"Your Excellency," he started. "We have come for advice."

An eye opened. A piercing, shrewd eye, without the beak being withdrawn from the wing.

Hamster noticed that he was being observed. "And so we came to you, for who else has the wisdom to meet this challenge?" He was beginning to become more eloquent.

The eye blinked. But the Crow did not stir.

"It's like this," and so Hamster outlined, as best he could, the threat of development that now hung over the north-east corner of the Heath. He spared no detail in order to make his case, and it is just possible that he embroidered the danger a little, but who could blame him, with so much at stake?

Finally he finished and fell silent.

After what seemed an age, the Crow withdrew his beak and reached down to preen what should have been his breast feathers,

18

but was now little more than pink flesh covered with a little stubble and down.

"Saaaow. Well, well, well. And saaow from these small ones caaames news! Haaaow, haaow, haaaow!" His hoarse laughter rang around the nest and was echoed by his many followers.

It was clearly a good joke. Finally the laughter ended and the eye was fixed on the two in the nest.

"You need advice. Advice. And saaow you come to us. And we will give it."

Vole extracted his notebook, and looked expectantly at the Crow.

"Advice, yes. But it will not be easy to follow. Aaaoh no! It is this: the danger will be stopped when the fountain runs clear. When the rust is no more, the houses will retreat! Yeeaaahs, they will!"

And with that he thrust his beak under what passed for a wing, and closed his eye. The interview was at an end.

* * *

The two friends picked themselves up from the grass onto which they had been so rudely deposited. Before them—in the distance—were the lawns rising gradually towards the imposing facade of Kenwood House. Its cream walls glowed in the sunshine like some discreetly decorated wedding cake.

"All very mysterious," said Vole, as he thumbed through his notebook, to check whether he'd got down what little the Crow had given in the way of advice.

"Hmmm," replied Hamster. It was a long trek back to their homes and they had little left to eat.

Off they strode, past the pond and the wooden bridge that appeared to span it. They had taken the path by the stream, to make sure they didn't lose their way home. Neither said a word, determined to put as much distance behind them as they could before the light went.

It was already fading, when suddenly Vole stopped dead in his tracks. "There it is!" he exclaimed, pulling on Hamster's rucksack and nearly toppling him backwards.

"What d' you mean?" he asked crossly.

"There! There! The rust on the fountain!"

So it was. A fountain, splashing at the foot of the hill, poured from a grimacing face set about with laurels. Hamster had seen it before, but had never taken much notice. Its strange decorations had always left him feeling a little odd, and he'd passed on by as soon as possible. But Vole was right. The water ran red with a rusty sort of substance, discolouring the stone and leaving peculiar pools that soaked away into the grass.

"But how?" he said. "How can stopping the rust stop the developers?"

And to that neither of them had any answer.

* * *

They made their way into Hamster's home as the church on the hill tolled two in the morning.

Both were absolutely exhausted; their feet swollen with walking, their backs weary from carrying their packs. Above all they were famished. As Hamster cut into a fruitcake he had been saving for an occasion (and what was this, if it wasn't?) Vole made a fire to warm their feet.

"Oooh!" said Hamster, as he sank into his green chair, while Vole made himself comfortable on a large cushion, covered with a kelim, on the floor.

The perplexing images of their journey rose before them as they stared into the flickering fire. Speech was beyond them and soon they nodded off, Hamster with his head sunk into his chest and Vole sprawled across the cushion.

* * *

They woke stiff and still groggy from their exertions. Hamster made a large breakfast with plenty of tea, toast and Seville marmalade and after a while they began to feel a good deal better. They took some of his old deck chairs and pitched them outside the entrance to catch the morning sun.

There they remained for the best part of two hours, drinking more tea and tossing ideas between them. But try as they might they could see no connection between the fountain, the rust and the development. Hamster had just declared, "I don't know. I just don't know," for the fourth time when he was interrupted by a voice from above.

"Give it a rest, will you! Been grinding on and on for hours, you have!"

It was Squirrel. Sitting in the fork of a tree above them he had heard them drone on without making an iota of progress and was thoroughly fed up.

Hamster spluttered in their defence, but Squirrel would have none of it.

"It's as plain as your face," (which both of the terrestrials thought was very rude.) "Find out why the fountain runs with rust and you're home and dry!"

"Well, of course we are," said Hamster crossly. "But where do we find that from?" his grammar getting tangled up in his anger.

"If it's the underground you need to get the gen on – it's the moles you want!" And with that Squirrel had had enough and bounded off over the trees in search of nuts and a quieter life.

* * *

The two friends sat around Hamster's well-worn kitchen table. On it stood a jug of lemonade, bread and a selection of cheeses. Now Vole was especially fond of cheese and happy to tuck in, when Hamster raised the question that had been in both of their minds.

"The moles. Do you think we can do business with them?"

It was a tricky one. Moles were all very well, unless they tunnelled under your very foundations. But they were so, well, so busy. Never a moment to spare. How could one get their attention, let alone their co-operation in the project? Vole told his host that hunger was a distraction from thought, and so they tucked in and said little until they were done.

Then Vole said, as they were clearing away: "Well, you know, there might just be a way. Do you remember the stories of what happened when Winston Churchill died?"

Hamster frowned. Of course he remembered the tales of the funeral, but how on earth could that throw any light on events? "Go on."

"They all came out. At midnight. And with the smallest at the front, and the largest at the rear they paraded to the top of Parliament Hill two abreast with a Union Jack at the front."

"Yes, yes," said Hamster. It had been the talk of the Heath down the years.

"So there's no doubting their patriotism, their love of home and hearth and all that," said Vole. "All we have to do is dress this problem in the right colours and they'll back us to the hilt."

Hamster put down the plates he was carrying and went over and gave Vole a hug. "What a fellow you are! What a fellow! Not just a note-taker at all! You've cracked it!"

* * *

Hamster led the way. He was a little stout around the middle – "well set," as he explained to himself and he puffed as they got to the top of the hill overlooking the ponds.

It was a lovely day. The grass was full of daisies as they made their way along the plateau towards the knot of oaks that was, by reputation, the centre of the mole universe.

Now it's important to explain that although moles may look like simple little folk, they come from an extraordinarily complex social background. What may look like no more than a small pile of untidy earth to you or me is, in reality, the outward sign of an intricate network of burrows, tunnels, passages, cellars and stores. In fact, it is only the military discipline of the moles that keeps it all in first class working order.

Hamster let Vole make the initial contacts since, he argued, they were cousins of sorts. "But they loathe water!" Vole protested.

"Never mind!" said Hamster, always a little reticent about introductions.

So Vole walked towards the nearest molehill until he was about a foot from it. And then, in the manner dictated by the codes of etiquette he had read, he knocked politely on the ground three times.

Nothing happened. Vole stepped forwards and repeated the exercise. This time the hill burst open and an angry head poked out. "Now then, now then! What's all this about? Got no manners have we? Can't wait for a reply? Just knock away!"

"Terribly sorry," tried Vole, but Hamster pushed him out of the way. "My friend was a little over anxious," he said. "Very important business you see."

The mole, who was straightening his cap on his head, looked distinctly unimpressed and was just about to disappear again when Hamster put on his best stage voice, and said at the top of his whisper, "National Security!"

"Oh." said the mole, still unimpressed, but looking a little more respectful. "Oh, well. Then perhaps you'd better follow me."

And so it was that first Hamster then Vole disappeared beneath the turf, leaving the blue sky and the warm breezes to their own devices.

* * *

Down the tunnels they went. The mole darted ahead, familiar with the twists and turns they were following. Hamster and Vole did their best to keep up, but every now and then they found the mole waiting impatiently at a fork, hands on hips.

Everywhere there was a bustle of activity. Some moles were repairing the walls, others dragging sacks full of earth from new diggings. Still others were busy in store rooms that led off the main passageways, counting, cleaning and checking.

Roots penetrated the tunnel roof, but were neatly tied out of the way by giant hawsers. Structures were reinforced by steel girders, held together with bolts the size of your fist. Pipes channeled water, that would otherwise have leaked into the passages, into drains in the floor, where it disappeared with a gurgle.

They had travelled for nearly twenty minutes when the tunnel turned a sharp bend and opened out. Before them lay a hall of quite extraordinary proportions. They had by now become used to the dim light and low ceilings the moles seemed to prefer, but this was very different.

The roof was three times a mole's height, supported by huge hammer beams carved in intricate design, showing episodes from the country's heroic past. Spread out before them was a large table, with the complex of tunnels drawn in minute detail. Junior moles stood around the table's edge moving models through the maze. Each represented a particular activity. Some were lines of soil being moved to the surface. Others were trains of food being transported to store rooms.

Vole was fascinated, scribbling away in his notebook until a rather officious looking mole came up to him and tapped on his shoulder. "Strictly secret!" he said ominously, snapping Vole's notebook closed. Vole looked sheepish but didn't argue.

"Follow me," the officious mole instructed and they trooped off behind him to a glass office suspended over the floor of the hall.

* * *

They were led before a panel of moles. Now all moles look very much alike, to outsiders that is. And these were no different. But there was something about their bearing that seemed to single them out from the rest. They all wore caps, but the mole in the middle wore one with a little gold braid around the edge. Not very conspicuous, but evidently some insignia designating rank.

"Now then," he said. "What's all this about national security? Not a phrase to bandy about lightly."

He looked stern, but Hamster reminding himself that he had seen the Crow only days before, so he took courage, drew himself up and held forth.

"I am sure you will agree," he began, "that what we have here"— and at this point he waved his hand in the general direction of the table below them—"represents a national asset." The moles said nothing, but he felt that at least their stares were not hostile.

"We have learnt of a plan. A plan that would endanger a significant proportion of the Heath. And since the Heath is, by general consent, one of the glories of the kingdom any attack on it is de facto an attack on the very lifeblood of our country!"

It was a little overblown, but Hamster had been practising in front of his mirror.

So he told them what he had heard. Of the dastardly plan to lop off a corner of the Heath. Just when he thought their attention might be drifting, he added that he suspected a foreign power was behind the scheme, taking the opportunity to describe the Dutchman and his cigar.

Hamster thought he had given a thoroughly convincing performance, complete with theatrical gestures. So he was rather taken aback when all the central mole said was, "You will withdraw," and they were marched out of the office and sent to wait in a corner of the hall.

"Well," said Hamster. "Well, I just don't know! What are they playing at? Don't they recognise danger when it's in front of their nose?"

Vole laid a comforting paw on his friend's arm. "Don't worry. They didn't dismiss it. We'll just have to be patient." And with that he re-opened his notebook and went back to making sketches, keeping one eye on the moles round the table who were far too busy to give the two strangers a second glance.

* * *

They were soon back in the glass office.

"We have considered your report," declared the most senior mole. "It tallies with intelligence of our own, although it seems a little exaggerated in parts."

Hamster felt aggrieved, but let it pass.

"Accordingly, I have detailed my aide de camp to accompany you to draw a proper assessment of the situation," he continued. "Then, and only then, will we decide on the appropriate response."

Hamster would have protested that it was urgent, but felt his remarks might not receive the weight they deserved. Instead he replied, "Very well. We will take your aide de camp back to our home. The Dutchman talked of a site visit tomorrow. So if we set off before daybreak, we should be in place when their party turns up. Then your mole can see for himself!"

31

The head mole nodded, and with that one of the moles to his right got up and led them out of the hall. "Just need to get a bit of kit," Mole said as they stopped outside a small door on the side of the tunnel. Inside was the smallest bedroom you might imagine. There was a dark green bunk on one side, with a desk beneath it. There was only one chair, and the walls were lined with charts and drawings of sections of the Heath and the kinds of vehicles to be found on it, in elevation and profile. Not an inch of space was wasted. The only indication that this was inhabited by anyone in particular was a small, silver frame, containing the photograph of a young mole, who was female and pretty, in a moleish sort of way.

From a tin trunk under the desk, the mole drew out a rucksack, evidently pre-packed, ready for any occasion. Into it he slipped a water bottle and another parcel that looked remarkably like a holster to Vole. "That's the lot," he said, and led them down another set of tunnels.

The tunnels went down, down, down. At first the two friends thought they were simply burrowing into the hill. Then it became clear that they were travelling in a specific direction. Every now and then the mole consulted small brass plaques placed next to junctions, before plunging on with even greater vigour. Finally, and just when Hamster had had about enough of all this twisting and turning down dank passages, up they popped out into the fresh air.

There they were, much to his surprise, not two grass clumps from his own burrow. "Well! And to think I never noticed that entrance!" he thought. But he kept it to himself. Moles were sufficiently puffed up with self importance as it was. So he invited them both into his burrow in what he considered to be his most hospitable manner.

* * *

The following day the going was hard. Mole had shown them another short cut down a tunnel that took them a good way towards the rusty spring. But from there on it had been a long slog. Up the grassy slope they had gone and down to the stream, which they crossed with some difficulty. Leaving the spring to their left (Hamster was pleased not to pass too close to the spout with the grinning head) they made their way up a steep bank and into a great meadow that seemed to stretch as far as the eye could see.

The meadow was dotted with hawthorn and they sat beneath one to eat a breakfast of egg mayonnaise sandwiches as the sun rose over the distant trees. Egg mayonnaise sandwiches were Vole's favourite and he'd been deputed to rustle up provisions while the other two plotted their journey the night before. Mole looked warily at the sandwich he was offered: not quite military fare, but he ate three nonetheless. Walking was hungry work.

After breakfast Hamster led the way. "You see that path?" he asked his companions from the top of a tussock of grass. The narrow path crossed the meadow ahead, rising from a branch of the stream on their left and disappearing into the distance on their right. "Well, it's along here that they'll come. The question is, how will we know where they'll stop to discuss their plans?"

"If I was them," said Mole, "I would stop where the path is at its highest or lowest point. At maximum and minimum elevations, as we say. From there the best views are to be had. So if we send Vole to the stream's edge and we head north for the high ground, we should cover both possibilities."

It seemed sensible. So although Vole felt a little out of it, he trudged off towards the stream, with instructions to signal with a pocket mirror if the Dutchman passed that way.

Now they were not certain when exactly the meeting was planned. All three found what cover they could. Vole under the stream's bank, where he felt quite at home; Mole and Hamster under some brambles that grew by the side of the path.

It was a long wait and Mole was looking at his watch (irritatingly) for the umpteenth time when a flash appeared through the bramble stalks. "That's it!" he cried. "Vole's signal! They're on their way."

Not five minutes later came the crunch of heavy footsteps up the path. They grew nearer but there was no sound of talking. Mole and Hamster huddled beneath their brambles, hoping against hope that they would stop. Just as the footsteps were almost upon them, there was a wizz and a missile, spewing smoke, almost landed on top of them. It was the Dutchman's cigar, spat out as he wheezed his way up the gentle incline.

"Ya!" he exclaimed to his unseen companion. "Now you see it! But vot a site!"

Hamster and Mole, gradually enveloped in stale smoke, could hardly believe their luck.

* * *

Back in the glass gallery at the heart of the mole empire, Hamster and Vole sat back watching with excited satisfaction as Mole briefed his superiors.

"High density housing, with a Mediterranean flavour to provide an illusion of space by means of a series of interlocking, juxtaposed courtyards and blocks." Mole had noted the Dutchman's words with the precision of a trained military mind. With ruthless efficiency he outlined the depth of the catastrophe now facing them all. A five acre site, laid out on the slope to the east of the spring. "To maximise the number of units and thereby the profitability of the exercise, " he concluded.

The whole description had been too chilling for Hamster. It had been reeled off as if the developer were talking of some remote stretch of the Algarve to be concreted over, and not their sacred Heath. He had felt as if a load of bricks was being showered down on them as they crouched beside the path, listening to the details tumble over them. "It can't be, it can't." he'd murmured.

He hadn't been the only one with doubts. The financier, for that was who the Dutchman's companion turned out to be, said the scheme was all very well, but how would it ever get planning permission?

At this the Dutchman positively preened. "Ach! A masterstroke! The City of London now runs dis place," he said with a dismissive sweep of his hand. "Vun account on de Cayman Islands vos all it took!" And he winked in a know-what-I-mean sort of way. And at this he had started off down the path, spilling details and enthusiasm for the project in his wake, with his financier in tow.

* * *

"It is," said the chief mole, "A situation as serious as anything we've ever faced. You were," and here he nodded towards Hamster and Vole "quite right to alert us to it. No doubt about it. I apologise for my incredulity. Too much hyperbole around these days. Got to guard against it. But this is different. We must plan. We must act!"

Hamster was quite taken aback. The resolve of the moles seemed so sudden, their conversion so complete. "Well," he said. "Well, it seems to me that you might be better placed than we are to take the lead in this affair. So much more used to strategy and things than Vole and I." He gestured towards his friend.

"Quite, quite," the chief mole assented. "Now you said the Crow predicted that they would be foiled when the fountain runs clear. Hmmmm. All very puzzling. Any ideas?"

At this he turned to the collected assembly, the twenty or so moles that made up the inner cabinet, together with Hamster and Vole. None stirred, until finally one mole at the back of the room put up his hand.

"Excuse me sir, but we in Planning were just thinking," and here he broke off.

"Yes, yes. Speak up!"

"We were just thinking," the mole from Planning continued. "If the fountain ran clear it would be because the rust was blocked off. Now the rust is the product of water passing over specific geological formations. If water from this source was removed, the water would be clear." Here he halted again, apparently feeling a little sheepish about stating the obvious.

"Clear, yes," said the chief mole. "But how would it benefit us? Is it just superstition?"

"Well, it might not be" said the planning mole, fishing a detailed map out of a satchel. "You see sir, we know that some of the water for the fountain drains from the slope upon which the houses are to be built. Here and here, " he indicated on the map for all to see.

"If we blocked the water source, it would back up. The ground would become saturated, marshy and quite unsuitable for building upon. I haven't done all the calculations, but in theory it might work."

Hamster was on his feet. "What insight! What a plan!" Vole had to restrain him with a tug on the sleeve.

"Quite," said the chief mole, looking none too happy about an outsider taking over his meeting with such an outburst of enthusiasm. "But we are overlooking something. How might it be done? Brilliant as the scheme might be, blocking a stream would require earth moving beyond even our abilities!"

"Begging your pardon, sir." This time it was an ancient looking mole, who rested on a stick. "Are we not forgetting something, something I am not sure I can mention in this company?"

"We are among friends," the chief mole declared, and Hamster and Vole glowed with satisfaction.

"Very well then," and at this he cleared his throat. "It's our stockpile of last resort. Long forgotten by some. But not by all. We have guarded it closely all these years, against an occasion like this. I mention it only with your permission, but desperate times do seem to call for desperate measures!"

"Ah," said the chief mole. "I understand your reticence. Very proper. But what is the use of a weapon that rusts in its scabbard?"

He looked round, and the assembly nodded assent, except for Hamster and Vole, who looked perplexed.

"You don't follow, do you? Well, it does go back a very long way. Before our days, and the days of our ancestors. To the times of the last great war." A hush had descended over the room. "You had better be shown," he said. And at this he indicated what he intended to Mole, who had become their companion.

* * *

Hamster and Vole had already been impressed by the tunnels they had been down but now their astonishment knew no bounds at what was revealed. Out of the great chamber, down a passage they came across a small door in the wall. It was painted dark brown and blended into the colour of the moist soil around it. On closer inspection it was revealed to be a mighty construction, so full of bolts and metal brackets it appeared indestructible. Mole tapped on it in code: four slow blows followed by three short ones.

In a moment it swung back on well-oiled hinges, to reveal a mole in battledress, pointing a gun at them.

"I come with this permission," Mole declared, handing the guard a letter with a large wax seal embossed upon it.

The guard looked at it with care, then drew back without a word, allowing the party of three to enter the tunnel.

It was narrower than any they had been down so far. Worse than that, it ran uphill almost without pause. Hamster, and even Vole, had difficulty keeping up with Mole whose energy seemed boundless. Curving only around boulders and giant tree roots, the tunnel otherwise stretched straight ahead of them endlessly.

Finally, after what seemed like the best part of a day's march, the three came to another door. It was a welcome relief after their long journey. This door was built in the same fashion as the one they had left so very far behind. This time there was no guard. Instead Mole pulled a long key from his pocket and turned it in the lock.

As the door opened, the two companions gasped. Before them were stacked, what appeared to be enough munitions to start a small war. Shells of all descriptions, some standing in rows, others bolted to the floor or to the walls by wooden staves. Box after box marked 'grenades' or 'ammunition'. Rifles in neat stacks. A real arsenal.

Hamster and Vole stood and gazed in amazement.

* * *

Hamster finally found words. "Where? I mean, when? How did you get these?"

Mole looked quietly pleased by their surprise.

"Once men thought these islands would be overrun. They planned for resistance. Fight them on the beaches, that sort of thing. And more than just planned! They laid up stores to resist. The Home Guard they were called. Munitions. Explosives. Rations. All that was required to fight off the enemy!"

"The threat first receded, then passed," he continued. "Stores were uncovered and removed. Peace came and war seemed long gone. But, as we moles say, once placed, twice forgotten! How often are things stored and left behind?"

"But I digress," he said. "We marked on our maps every store as it was laid down. And each as it was moved. When it was all over, one remained! This one, believe it or not, is buried beneath the lawn by the great house at Kenwood: somewhere between the summerhouse and that ghastly statue. We have saved it against such a day as this. Always vigilant. Never allowing it to be disturbed!" He turned with evident pride towards his horde.

Hamster still looked puzzled, and said, "but what's this got to do with the problem in hand?" But before Mole could answer, Vole chipped in. "The explosives! Don't you see? With these you might blast the earth to block the stream beneath the ground, before it reaches the fountain red with rust!"

"Exactly," said the mole.

"How did you know?" whispered Hamster to his friend. But Vole just looked superior.

* * *

So the plans were laid. A permanent watch was established on the slope to the east of the fountain. Comings and goings noted with care: especially the measurements that were being taken mostly at night by the Dutchman's surveyors and engineers, who peered and poked and measured at the tussocks of grass over which they had such dastardly designs.

Hamster, eating a late tea with Vole puzzled over these comings and goings from the depths of his favourite green leather armchair. "I mean, why at night? Why in the dark?" he said.

"Obvious really," replied Vole, polishing off the last of the crumpets. This kind of remark really annoyed Hamster, but he'd learned to put up with it. "Just Vole's way really," he said to himself and waited.

"Surprise, you see," Vole continued. "The whole scheme depends on it. Unless it can be sprung on the world as a fait accompli, all will be lost. The row would be colossal. Will be anyway, but once there are 'facts on the ground', so to speak, what can be done? The foundations will be laid. Permission will have been given. Even if it were halted the Dutchman and his cronies would be quids in. Compensation would run into millions."

"I suppose so." Hamster said, still puzzled over how Vole knew so much.

Somehow the crumpets and teacakes seemed less than appealing, almost as if their scrumptiousness was undermined by the impending doom. After all, once the housing spread down one slope, where would it all end? The two friends looked out over the pond in front of them. A great crested grebe was swimming serenely, a V forming in its wake. The sun was going down. It seemed too perfect to last.

"Well," said Vole at last. "If anyone can pull it off, the moles can. We must trust their energy and their planning!"

Hamster stared out, saying nothing, the fading light matching his mood.

* * *

There then followed weeks and months of careful observation.

The moles, with their usual thoroughness, built tunnels and dugouts up to the edge of the site. It was a tremendous work, all carried out under what the moles called 'war conditions', meaning that the tunnels were constructed without producing mole hills, or spoil tips, as the moles called them. Instead, the earth was carried in small panniers out of the area, to be dumped in the rear away from prying eyes.

Hamster and Vole watched the proceedings with fascination and ranks of moles laboured day and night to complete the project.

"So busy. So active," said Hamster, as yet another team brushed past them in a tunnel just north of the last great pond, their trolleys packed with excavating equipment. "Mmmm," agreed Vole, peering out of an observation post that had been pushed up through a thicket of hazel.

It was now autumn. The ground before them was pale grey and brown as the frost killed off the grass. Tracks had appeared on the site, but there was little else to show for all the activities of the Dutchman and his allies. And even these seemed to have diminished in recent weeks.

"It's all a bit quiet for my liking," observed Vole, mumbling into his whiskers a little. "Calm before the storm?"

"Or perhaps they've had second thoughts?" wondered Hamster.

But Vole simply replied with one of his "Mmmms" and stared out across the tussocks of grass.

* * *

The blow fell when they were least expecting it.

Indeed, even the moles were caught off guard. All the elaborate preparation and earthworks would have been for nought if it hadn't been for the squirrel. He'd come bounding down to the lookout point in which Hamster, Vole and Mole had taken to sleeping, rudely hammering on the window.

"Blimey! You going to doze through it all then?" yelled Squirrel, as Vole's head emerged sleepily through the curtains.

But before Vole could reply, Mole was up, through the door, and into the observation tower. When the others joined him, rather out of breath, he was already peering through the slit, his binoculars trained on the hillside before them.

Even without the binoculars, the sight was terrible to behold. There in the moonlight, their gleaming silver blades held high before them, three bulldozers advanced in a line. As the friends stared, the first lowered its blade, gouging a rut deep into the turf of the Heath.

"Not a moment to lose," shouted Mole, who set off down the stairs in the direction of the regional command post.

By the time Hamster and Vole reached it, Mole had already aroused the garrison. Everywhere moles scurried about, shouting orders down phone lines, moving models across maps, sending scouts to monitor the advance. But despite the activity, the outlook was bleak.

It was the mole with braid on his cap who summoned Hamster and Vole to an emergency summit. "Despite our best endeavours, we have been taken by surprise. Foolish really. We planned for a frontal attack, through the car park by Kenwood House. Our lookouts were there."

"Now," he said with great weariness, "they took us from the flank, simply crashed their way through the Heath fence, and advanced where we least expected them. With our explosives pre-positioned, we are left without defences. It will take at least an hour to move them. By that time all will be lost. The outline of the foundations will be in place."

Turning now to his colleagues, he placed his cap on the desk beside them. "I have failed you all. I resign my Commission and go now to take my place in the last trench."

Hamster looked hopefully towards Vole, but for once his friend had nothing to add.

* * *

"They fell upon the men in serried ranks," Hamster was fond of saying at this point of the story.

And down the years, as he made quite certain that the next generation of hamsters, voles, moles and all the others were fully informed of every twist and turn in this, the Heath's most glorious hour, Hamster always ensured that the phrase cropped up. It really didn't matter that none of them knew quite what "serried ranks" meant. It just sounded right.

Certainly, no-one on either side had been ready for help when it finally arrived. All had seemed quite hopeless as the bulldozers drove remorselessly onwards, the piles of broken turf and earth growing behind them.

The crows attacked with the moon behind them, diving directly onto the yellow bulldozers below. The men inside, who had been concentrating on the task at hand, had not the faintest idea what had hit them.

All of a sudden their vision was obscured by hundreds of outstretched wings. The cabins of their bulldozers were filled with fanning, beating wings. Their faces pecked by merciless beaks. Their hands attacked by sharpened claws.

In fear and amazement, without even turning off their machines, the men had fled from the field. Screaming in terror, waving their hands above their heads to keep off the savagery of the skies, they ran as if their lives depended upon it.

* * *

"Now is our chance!"

The chief mole, who had been crouching just feet from the advancing menace, jumped out of the trench, followed by his commandoes.

The engineering corps, which had been valiantly dismantling the charges they had set, so as to reposition them ahead of the menace, was reinforced. Hundreds of moles working in canvas harnesses pulled and coaxed their dangerous cargoes onto trolleys.

Ahead of them the demolition squad was working feverishly, digging new sites for the explosives. All caution was abandoned. Piles of earth were growing by the minute, as they dug into the side of the hill.

Time was not on their side.

By the fence, on the boundary of the Heath, the Dutchman was trying to muster his forces. "You pasetic, verseles men!" he yelled. "Haf you no kurridge? Shased by burds? Burds!"

"But they was crazy!" declared one driver—patting a deep scratch left on his cheek by a razor sharp beak.

It only made the Dutchman still angrier. "Idiots! Vot you sink? Burds go to keel you? If you don't get beck now—I keel you first!"

And with threats and promises of extra cash in their pockets, he gradually rallied his troops. Finally, they plucked up their remaining ration of courage and ran back to their machines, which were still growling where they had been left running, slamming the cabin doors shut.

But they were too late.

Just as the first crunched his engine into gear, the earth all around him erupted. Like a giant egg being flipped over in a frying pan, the bulldozer rose into the air and came down on its side.

From their observation post Hamster and Vole felt a huge wave of air pass over them, as the whole world seemed to roar in their ears. Picking themselves up, they peered out as the smoke and dust cleared.

In the moonlight the devastation seemed complete. One bulldozer lay on its side, another had turned over entirely. The third had dived head first into a gaping pit. Nothing stirred ahead of them, but far off, on the edge of the Heath, a bulky man got hastily into a car and flung a smoking cigar out of the window as he drove off in haste.

* * *

The great hall had seen many splendid occasions, but nothing quite like this.

The moles had gone to extraordinary lengths to celebrate the victory. The walls were hung with banners of battles long past. The tables shone with regimental silver. The floor had been strewn with herbs and flowers.

And everywhere there was food. Whole cheeses on sideboards. Wild mushroom pates to make your mouth water. Soups of exquisite clarity. Aubergine soufflés. A train of moles appeared bearing individual tomato quiches. Beer flowed from barrels and wine from gallon jars.

In the centre, Hamster and Vole were seated on either side of the commander-in-chief, who had been restored to rank, with a new campaign medal on his ceremonial uniform.

"It was," he was just explaining to them in turn, "a case of fighting the last battle once again." Despite the success they were celebrating, he was evidently still smarting from being taken by surprise. "No-one ever envisaged an attack from the rear."

"The price of linear thinking," observed Vole.

"Quite, quite," agreed the moles' commander as he passed some excellent stuffed pepper to Hamster who wondered, as ever, how his friend managed to be so well informed?

The old Crow was guest of honour, and special mention was made of his now famous prediction. It was sagely observed that the fountain did now run clear, even though its flow had diminished. Crow was given the Freedom of the Heath, by acclamation, an honour he accepted by taking his beak from under his withered wing and nodding gracefully to the assembled mass. Hamster and Vole were also mentioned and special presentation goblets given to them, with the words 'Ever Vigilant' engraved upon them.

When the last toast had been drunk and the last thanks been given, Hamster and Vole made their way out of Mole Hall, and started rather groggily down the path towards home. They crossed the great meadow and reached the hedge on the other side, which was full of wild roses. In the distance the clouds were touched with fire, as the sun said his own farewell.

Vole steadied Hamster as they made their way over the log that crossed the stream. They were nearly home before either of them spoke.

"Well," said Hamster as they prepared to part. "Well, now that's what I call a real adventure. Haven't had one of those in a long time!"

Vole watched him as he turned and stumbled over the root, past the rock, and into his burrow. "No," he said fondly to himself. "Not since you raced up the curtain and flung yourself through the window, hoping for the best. And that was a very long time ago!"

And with that, Vole went back to his boats.